THE SECRET DIARY OF A TIME TRAVELLING CAT

Nannette L. He

Cover cat photo © Katosu
http://fav.me/dxz9vu
http://www.youtube.com/katosu

To my parents; and to Tracey Eva Edwards – thanks for believing I can do it.

TABLE OF CONTENTS

CHAPTER 1

London, England, September 1666

I curled up in a ball at the foot of Master Pepys bed. He kept tossing and turning, which disturbed my comfortable position. I therefore decided to teach him a lesson by sitting on his chest with my paw resting on his open, snoring mouth. This had the desired effect of waking him with a start. He stared into my bright green eyes and pushed me away.

'Oh Tom, why do you keep waking me so?'

He leapt out of bed, smoothed down his white night shirt and lit a candle.

Feeling sorry for him, I rubbed against his ankles and purred. He ran his hand down the tabby fur on my back and scratched the side of my face, just below my whiskers. I purred extra loudly to show my appreciation. He knew my favourite stroking places.

Suddenly a great scream came from the street below: 'Fire! Fire!'

Master Pepys rushed to the window and looked out. I jumped up to the window ledge and saw below great crowds of people rushing around shouting and screaming. In the distance was a huge fire, gradually getting closer to our house. St Pauls Cathedral was a ball of flames and sparks flew up into the night sky.

'Tom, we must escape from here', he said. 'But first I must bury the most important, valuable items in the garden – starting with my prize cheese.'

I watched in amazement as he rushed downstairs to prepare his cheese for burial.

'Surely I'm the most important, valuable item you possess' I wanted to say, but Master Pepys was too busy to notice me in all the commotion.

At this point Mrs Pepys woke up and joined her husband in ordering the servants around, screaming, crying and stepping on my tail. I crept under the bed and decided to stay there until everyone calmed down. But then Master

Pepys started shouting for me, saying it was most urgent that I joined him. Feeling a little warmer than usual, I realised he was probably right, so I made an appearance, only for him to scoop me up in his arms and rush downstairs with me.

Outside the house was a large cart full of various items belonging to Mr & Mrs Pepys. We climbed aboard the cart and a horse pulled us along. Some people went to the nearest fields – Moorfields and Lincoln's Inn Fields, but Pepys said it would be safer to go further, so we travelled until we reached the highest ground – Parliament Hill on Hampstead Heath. From here I could look down at London below, which was by now completely covered in huge flames.

Master Pepys squeezed me tightly and said 'We had a lucky escape there Tom'.

The Hill was full of people, surrounded by all their belongings. Everyone stared in amazement as London burnt down. Some people were stunned and looked like they were sleep-walking. Others were crying as they watched their houses being destroyed by flames.

One man wiped his eyes with a handkerchief, turned to Master Pepys and said, 'How was the City when you left it?'

Pepys replied: 'I ran through Watling Street and every creature was coming laden with goods to save and here and there six people carried away in beds. Everyone was saving themselves and their possessions, not fighting the fire. They were all heading out to the fields of Islington, Finsbury, Highgate. St Pauls Cathedral was a miserable site. The roof and choir fallen in. A ruin. Even the pigeons were reluctant to leave their perches and hovered about until they burned their wings and fell down.' Tears sprung into Master Pepys eyes and he wiped them with a handkerchief. 'When the Lord Mayor was first told of the fire, he said: "Pish! A woman might piss it out!" and went back to bed. The King commanded me to order the Lord Mayor to pull down houses in the path of the fire, but when I reached him and gave him the Kings orders he said: "Lord what can I do? I am spent, people will not obey me. I have been pulling down houses but the fire overtakes us faster than we can do it."'

As Pepys carried on talking, I started to wander around, seeing if I could find anything to eat. I spotted a mouse, so I used my highly successful hunting technique, the secret weapon being surprise, surprise, surprise (I can't emphasise enough the importance of surprise here). I lowered my body as close to the ground as possible, and crept forward, slowly, slowly, slowly. Being a tabby cat has the advantage that I can usually camouflage myself and blend into the background. I chuckled to myself, thinking 'that mouse is going to get a nasty surprise soon. Ha, ha, ha!' I was like a coiled spring, edging closer and closer to my target. Judging the right moment to pounce is a matter of instinct, wind direction, lighting, and huge intelligence. When I thought the time was right, I unleashed the full force of my body and hurtled forward like a cannon ball towards the unsuspecting mouse. Unfortunately for me, the mouse disappeared as soon as I reached it, but not one to be deterred by small facts like these, I chased after it. The mouse was running in-between everyone's feet, causing screams from women it passed by. I gave chase, but the mouse found some hidden venue to escape into, and I lost it. Damn!

Feeling very cheesed off by this mishap, I decided the best thing was to rest and try and recuperate, but finding a spot to lie down in was tricky, as the area was completely packed with people. Humans really do just get in the way sometimes, and there's nothing more annoying than humans getting in the way of a cat's most essential requirement – sleep. People think cats are lazy, but really all we are doing is conserving energy. I do everything with the minimum amount of effort required, and I have to think about waking up a long time before I actually do it.

I tried to find my way back to Master Pepys, as I thought he would be a nice cushion to lie on. It took quite awhile, but eventually I found him, and evidently he'd been trying to find me too. He was red in the face and sweating like a pig.

'Oh Tom, where have you been? I've been looking for you everywhere,' he said.

He grabbed hold of me and held me tightly against his chest. I licked the back of his hand and he kissed the top of my head.

Mrs Pepys had always been jealous of me, and she said: 'you think more of that cat than you do of me'.

Master Pepys sighed. 'Please don't start with your jealous accusations again,' he said.

'And of course it's not just the cat that you care more about either. I know all about your mistresses. There is gossip in all the city that you follow women in the street and try to grab them. One woman even told me you followed her into church and you tried to lay hands on her, but she guarded herself with a hat pin against your advances.' Mrs Pepys folded her arms across her chest, in readiness for war.

'I do not think this is the time or place to discuss matters of a personal nature. Surely we have more important things to think about now – like the destruction of our house and our city,' Master Pepys replied.

'Well, I want to discuss it now,' Mistress Pepys said.

Master Pepys shrugged his shoulders, let out a long sigh, lowered his head and said: 'The truth is, I do indulge myself a little the more in pleasure, knowing that this is the proper age of my life to do it, and out of my observation that most men that do thrive in the world do forget to take pleasure during the time that they are getting their estate, but reserve that till they have got one, and then it is too late for them to enjoy it...however, you hath something in your gizzard, that only waits an opportunity of being provoked to bring it up, but I will not, for my content-sake, give it.'

I could sense one of the Pepys long arguments coming on. It was time to batten down the hatches and take cover.

People had started to erect tents on Parliament Hill, and all the other places they had fled to – Moorfields, Lincoln's Inn Fields etc. We slept in a tent that night. The next morning Pepys said: 'I do not think Parliament Hill is a suitable place after all. It is too crowded. Let us get a boat and sail down to Woolwich.'

So we all boarded the horse and cart again and travelled back into the City. The fire was still raging. As we reached the riverside Pepys decided to visit the church next to the Tower of London - All Hallows Barking. Pepys took me with him as he climbed the steeple of the church. From here we saw great fires, oil cellars and brimstone and other things burning. There was one entire arch of fire in a bow up the hill above, a mile long. Riverside warehouses spewed wine and spirits into the river, and people were scurrying hither and thither, moving their possessions at the last minute from relative's house to relative's house as each in turn was threatened. There was a blaze at the Temple, Holborn and Cripplegate, where the King himself was seen helping the soldiers. Later the King rode out to the people camped in the fields and promised to supply them with bread.

After the visit to the church, Master and Mrs Pepys started to load up the boat that would take us to Woolwich, but as they were doing this, I spotted a mouse, so I decided to chase it. I lost the mouse eventually, so I decided to try and make my way back to our house. Perhaps I could dig up that cheese that Master Pepys had buried in the garden. I weaved in and out of the forest of legs in front of me but as I got closer to the centre of the City the heat became unbearable. Sparks landed on my back and singed my fur. My whiskers twitched and all my instincts told me this was not a good idea.

I was now in Fleet Street, so I went inside St Brides church, where Master Pepys was baptised. I walked down the stairs that led into the crypt below. It was very dark and smelt musty and damp. Slowly my eyes adjusted to the darkness and I could just about see. I let my whiskers guide me to a spot in the corner made up of very small red and yellow tiles, called tessarae. It reminded me of an ancient Roman mosaic floor, but looked more like a pavement. As I put my left paw on the floor, it suddenly lit up and the crypt and church around me disappeared. Now I was surrounded by people in ancient Roman clothes. My spine tingled and my fur stood on end as I realised I had been transported back through time to when Romans ruled London and the world, fifteen hundred years ago.

CHAPTER 2

London, England, September, 79 AD

I walked down Fleet Street – or rather, what used to be Fleet Street. The buildings that used to be there were now replaced by gaps of brown earth interspersed by small wooden huts. Some were shops, with large open fronts that faced the street. Others were take away food places or bars.

I looked to see where St Pauls Cathedral used to be and in its place was a large white building made of stone and marble – a Temple of Diana. The spot where St Brides church used to be was a Roman pavement, with a small white stone temple, enclosing a well. Around the temple were graves and headstones.

I felt quite bewildered and lost, but hunger concentrated my mind, and I headed towards the smell of food coming from a take away food place. Pizzas were being shovelled into a large oven, but I was more interested in the fish I saw lying on a counter. I waited until I thought no-one was looking, then I jumped up onto the bar, caught hold of the fish between my jaws and ran off. I heard a man shout and come after me, but I kept running as fast as I could, and I managed to shake him off. I took the fish round the back of a building, where I thought I wouldn't be disturbed, and devoured it. Delicious!

After this sumptuous feast I licked myself all over and curled up in a ball, ready for a nice sleep. But just as I was getting comfortable, a great noise and commotion disturbed my peace. I looked up and saw a large fat man on a horse riding down the street. I guessed he must be someone important as lots of people had lined the street and were cheering and applauding him.

In order to get away from the noise I nipped down a little alley and found I was next to the river Thames. It looked much wider than I could remember it. A boat was moored by the river bank, and men were loading it up with large barrels. I jumped on board the boat and found my way down into the hold where the barrels were stored. It was nice and warm down here, and once the men had finished and gone away, I curled up in a corner and went to sleep.

My rest didn't last long, as the boat started lurching and rolling around. I went back up on deck and could see it had set sail and was drifting down the river. Too late to get off now, so I went back in the hold and settled down to resume my sleep.

CHAPTER 3

Pompeii, Italy, 79 AD

I assumed it would be a short trip, but it was very, very long. After what seemed forever we eventually landed in Italy. I jumped off the boat and set my paws on Italian soil for the first time. The weather was a definite improvement on English weather. In England there is only one season – winter. Sometimes the winter is a bit mild, so people call it spring or summer, but really it is still winter – cold, cloudy, raining. In Italy it was hot and sunny.

As I walked inland I came across a town surrounded by a high brick wall. The sign above the gate said "Pompeii". I walked in and came across a maze of little streets with shops and houses. In the middle of the roads were stepping stones for people to cross the street if it was muddy. Carts pulled by donkeys crowded the roads. Eventually I came across a large open area – the Forum, with tall marble pillars and white stone temples with statues outside them.

The Forum was packed with people, standing around in groups talking, rushing to and fro, buying things from stalls. Everyone wore tunics or togas. It was strange to see men wear such dresses.

By this time I was sweating my fur off and in desperate need of a drink. I went down a little road which led off from the Forum. There were erect penises carved into the streets which seemed to point me in the direction I needed to go in. After following them for awhile I eventually came to a brothel. There were tiny little rooms in here, with men and women having sex and erotic paintings on the walls. Interesting as it sometimes is to watch humans having sex (mainly for its comedy value), I had more important things on my mind – like getting a drink. Everyone seemed too busy to notice me, although in one room there was a woman on her own, so I went in and gave her the full-on charm treatment – rubbing against her ankles, purring, meowing, looking pitifully into her eyes, until she relented and took me out the back where she gave me a bowl full of water and some fish.

Suddenly the ground started to shake. I ran outside and could see a nearby volcano called Vesuvius erupting. A pillar of ash spurted out of the volcano. I didn't want to hang around for the lava flow which I knew would follow. I quickly thought back to when I was transported through time before. How did it happen? All I did was step on a Roman pavement in the crypt of the church, and that transported me through time. I desperately needed the same thing to happen again, but I had no idea how to do it.

The sky became black as night. The earth started to shake again and everyone in the brothel ran outside. The women were screaming. Houses started to collapse around me. Maybe this was something I wasn't going to be able to escape or survive.

Pumice stones started to rain down. I ran under a cart for shelter. The noise of the stones hitting against the cart was unbearable. Gas, which smelt like rotten eggs, made my eyes water and burnt the back of my throat. I tried to swallow but my mouth felt like it was on fire. I shut my eyes and wished so hard to get away from here. Then suddenly everything went black and silent.

CHAPTER 4

London, England, 2020

When I opened my eyes, I was in the sitting room of a flat. A computer on a table was in one corner, and in another were a TV and CD player. Against the wall was an upright piano, sandwiched in-between large bookcases crammed full of books. On the walls hung framed prints of cats, sunsets, Italy, the South of France. A framed photo on the table showed a woman in her early 40s holding me in her arms. She was slim, with bright blue eyes and shoulder length chestnut brown hair. Stuck to the photo was a sticky note which said: "Louise & Tom – the Dynamic Duo".

The computer was on, so I sat in front of it. The screen showed an internet dating website. The profile photo showed a young, attractive Italian man with short black hair. In the section "About me", he'd written:

'Sometimes ... when you cry ... no one sees your tears... Sometimes... when you are in pain... no one sees your hurt... Sometimes... when you are worried.... no one sees your stress...Sometimes ... when you are happy ... no one sees your smile ......But try masturbating in Asda car park just one ****ing time & see how much ****ing attention you get. Can someone pick me up from the police station please ?'

I clicked the mouse to send him an email, when my owner Louise came in the room and said: 'Oh Tom, get your sweaty paws off my mouse.' She then lifted me away from the computer and plopped me on the floor.

I licked my tabby fur and curled up in a ball in the corner of the room for a rest. Surfing the net had exhausted me. But I could see out of the corner of my eye that Louise had become transfixed by the profile of the Italian man. She sent him an email and he replied straight away. I could sense another dating disaster waiting to happen.

Sure enough, a few days later, she stumbled into the flat with the Italian man and they proceeded to have wild, exhausting sex. I just sat in the corner and watched. I don't need to surf the net for porn, I can get a real live show in my flat for free.

On his profile he'd put that he just wanted to date and "wasn't looking for anything serious". 'That's the problem', Louise said to me, 'all these young, attractive men either aren't interested in me at all, or they just want to use me for casual sex. They're so attractive they can get anyone they want, so they have a long list of women to get through each week. The best men are married or gay; so it's rare that someone young, sexy and attractive emails me. Usually the guys that contact me look like freaks, weirdo's, thugs, psychos, nightclub bouncers. I've had men who want me to wear angora sweaters because they have a wool fetish, or men who want to dominate me or men who want me to dominate them. Or, I get emails from guys who are really ancient, ugly, boring, virgins, repressed homosexuals, mummies' boys, sexually incompetent, just want to be friends because they don't know how to have sex, or are too religious to have sex, or think it's too dirty and sordid, or are more interested in arranging their CDs into alphabetical order than in having sex. Why can't I find someone young, sexy and attractive who wants a serious relationship? And why can't I say no to being used for casual sex all the time?' She looked into my eyes like I knew the answer, but the inner workings of the human mind are a mystery to me. All I could do was put a reassuring paw on her shoulder as she held me in her arms.

'If only I could find a man who was like you', she said, 'affectionate, loyal, caring, supportive, sympathetic.' I hated to break it to her that the only reason I was hanging around was because she knew how to use a tin opener. If I could use a tin opener myself, I would be off like a shot. Although Louise did also provide me with warmth, as she always had the heating up full blast, and it was nice to be stroked. So yes, I admit, I got a few things from Louise that made me want to stay around, besides tuna.

I knew what the aftermath would be of sex with the Italian. And there she was before me a few days later, in a crumpled heap, with used, wet tissues all over the floor, sobbing her heart out. She opened her red, puffy eyes as I nuzzled her face, but this made her cry even more. In-between sobs she said: 'You're the only....person...I mean cat....that cares about me.....Why, why, WHY, did I sleep with him? I knew he only wanted to use me for casual sex. I knew I'd never hear from him again.'

I had heard this all before of course, as Louise never learnt from her mistakes, she just kept repeating them, and this fact made her even more annoyed with herself.

Eventually, she phoned a friend and talked for hours. The phrases "all men are bastards" and "I'm better off being single and celibate for the rest of my life anyway" kept popping up in the conversation.

Louise said to her friend: 'The problem is that I always fancy men who are young and very attractive and way out of my league. So either I experience unrequited love for men who aren't interested in me at all, or if they do want to sleep with me, it's only because they want a free prostitute and they just use me for casual sex and then dump me. So out of desperation I put up with second best and settle for men I don't fancy. With my last boyfriend we skipped the honeymoon period and went straight to the disappointment. The dream of romance is that you fall in love and live happily ever after; the reality is that you cling to each other like mould, despising each other until you split up. Now I realise it's better to be on your own than be with someone who makes you unhappy.

When you're a kid the first disillusionment is realising Father Xmas doesn't exist. When you're an adult the second disillusionment is realising the perfect man doesn't exist. But men are crap in bed anyway – they use no foreplay and they think the clitoris is a Greek island. So perhaps I'm better off being single and celibate. At least that way I can't get hurt. There are no decent men around, so there's no point wasting time looking for what doesn't exist.'

It offended me to hear Louise slag off the entire male population. Just because the human male was deficient in many areas – including sex, didn't mean male cats could be put in the same low class. The male cat was superior to the human male in many respects. In my younger days I was considered a veritable stud that could pleasure the female cat into ecstatic raptures until she was so overcome she almost fainted. Although I was older now, I still had the magic touch. I hadn't lost that sexual charisma that made female cats drool whenever they saw me.

It was at this point that I decided to get some air, so I went out the cat flap and roamed my usual patch, past the adjoining houses, down our street – called Hornyold Road (very appropriate!). I peered into the windows to see if anything interesting was happening or if there was any food waiting for my attention.

Through one window I could see someone was watching the Oxford and Cambridge boat race on TV. As the boats sailed past the finishing line I thought to myself: 'That was almost exciting.'

So far, so ordinary, until I suddenly saw through a window a sight very peculiar. A beautiful white cat, with different coloured eyes – one bright blue, the other amber. The cat was sitting upright on a chair, like a human, with its back straight and its legs in front of it. Its face was human like too and it stared into my eyes like it was looking into my soul. The cat then jumped off the chair and came out the cat flap.

'You've got to help me', the white cat said. 'I'm not really a cat, I'm a human trapped inside a cat's body.'

'Yeah right' I said, sceptically.

'I'm not joking about this. I was a human, then I died and my soul was reincarnated inside this cat. A lot of cats are reincarnated humans, but with most of them they forget they used to be a human and so they become fully cat like, but the reincarnation didn't work properly with me, and I'm still partly human.'

My first thought was that the cat was insane, but then if she was telling the truth, it would explain why she sat like a human.

'Well I'd like to help you, but what can I do?' I said.

'I don't know,' the cat looked down at the floor and seemed very depressed.

'What's your name?' I asked.

'Crystal' she replied. 'What's yours?'

'Tom...You know sometimes you have to accept what you can't change, and since you can't change back to a human, maybe you should just embrace your catness and accept it.'

'But it's not that easy. It feels so strange being a cat. There are so many things I can't do now, that I could do before as a human,' Crystal said.

'But look at all the advantages of being a cat,' I replied. 'Humans have to go to work – get up early, commute on packed trains like animals being taken to slaughter, sit in an office all day with people they hate, do boring or stressful jobs they hate, be bullied by their bosses or workmates. The end result is that they're constantly tired, depressed, and have no time to do anything they want to do. They have to do this their whole life, until they retire, and then they have a few years of rest before they drop dead. What kind of life is that? Plus if they live in Britain they also have the added misery of constant crap weather – cold and rain all year round. And if they lose their job and become unemployed, they have to try and exist on benefits which are so low it's impossible to live on them. Plus the Government are scrapping the welfare state so there won't be any benefits at all soon, and then it'll be like Victorian times, when the poor were sent to the workhouse. Whereas think of all the advantages of being a cat – you can sleep ALL THE TIME – with the occasional break for food, drink, grooming and sex, of course And you get to be stroked and massaged by humans, cosseted, in front of the warmth of a cosy fire, or sunbathe in a beautiful garden or in front of a nice big window. Being a cat is SO much better than being a human. And if you can find a really good owner, someone who'll really pamper you, you've hit the jackpot and it's a never ending life of luxury and relaxation. Humans would love to be cats if they had the chance, and now you've been given that opportunity. Embrace it my friend! Celebrate being a cat! Vive le chat!'

'What?' Crystal asked.

'It's French for 'long live the cat'. I thought most cats spoke French, it is such an elegant, feline language.' I replied

'Well, I don't speak French. It's hard enough for me to speak cat. I know you are right though. I have to accept what I can't change, and I can't change the fact that I'm a cat, so I have to see the positive advantages to it.'

'Plus you are such a beautiful cat too, if I may say so.'

Crystal bowed her head in embarrassment. I went over to her and kissed her, and I was just about to do something more strenuous when I heard a loud bang.

I looked behind me and saw smoke coming from my flat. I ran as fast as I could until I got home. Louise was lying on the floor. The gas cooker had exploded and bits of it were scattered everywhere. I went over to Louise and nuzzled her. I didn't know if she was dead or just unconscious, but she didn't respond.

In the corner of the kitchen there was a big orange glow, like the sun. I walked up to it – expecting it to be hot and burn me, but it didn't. The more I stared at it the more hypnotised I felt. Something made me want to walk into the light, so I slowly approached it. I cautiously let the tip of a whisker go into the light. I wasn't burnt or singed, so I slowly put a paw inside. Seemed to be OK, no ill effects, so I walked into the light. It was so bright I had to shut my eyes.

CHAPTER 5

Cesena, Italy, 1502

I opened my eyes and to my amazement I was still alive, but somewhere different. I was now in a dark room. Sitting at a table was an old man with a long, white beard and long grey hair. His face was etched with lines and bags sat under his eyes. He was dressed shabbily in a loose, long white linen shirt and light brown woollen tights, called hose. Hunched over a drawing he was making, he seemed tired and weighed down with problems. A candle sat next to him on the table, creating the only spot of light in the room. Specks of dust floated in the candlelight.

He was so engrossed in his drawing that he didn't notice me for a long time, but eventually he saw me out of the corner of his eye and he stared at me in surprise. Beneath his thick, bushy eyebrows were bright, piercing blue eyes, and they now turned their full attention on me. His face softened as he looked at me, and he got up and came over to where I was sitting. He picked me up, sat me on his lap and started to stroke me. As he ran his hand across the tabby fur on my back and tickled me under the chin, he said "where have you come from then?" I purred and rubbed the side of my face against his hand.

Eventually he put me down on the floor and started to draw a picture of me. He stared into my eyes and I stared into his for a long time. Then he said 'I know all about you'. I was puzzled by this and even more puzzled when he said 'you don't know who I am do you? My name is Leonardo da Vinci.'

'Well, yes, as a matter of fact, I have heard of you. Master Pepys was always talking about you,' I thought to myself.

'Ah, Samuel Pepys, yes I know all about him' he said.

I stared at Leonardo da Vinci in wide eyed amazement.

'How can you understand what I'm thinking?' I meowed.

'I understand all animals. I can read their thoughts, and the noises they make, like your meows, I can translate into human language. So I know perfectly well what you are saying to me and thinking.'

'But that's not possible,' I replied.

'Not many people have this ability, it is true, and the ones that do are usually locked up in mental hospitals or burnt as witches. I therefore keep this ability to myself and don't mention it to anyone.'

Suddenly a man entered the room. He had the face of a weasel – thin and narrow, with a sickly smirk. He had short black hair and was clean shaven, but with some stubble showing through. Wearing a large black cape with bright red sleeves, his hands were large and clutched in one of them was a glove, which he grasped like a pigeon he was strangling.

Leonardo Da Vinci froze when this man entered the room. Fear and tension flickered across his face.

'What brings you here Machiavelli?' Leonardo asked.

'The Prince, His Highness Borgia, wishes to see you', he replied.

'I'm honoured,' Leonardo said sarcastically. 'Perhaps he wishes to pay me?'

'I wouldn't get your hopes up on that score', Machiavelli said.

Leonardo put on a cloak and left the room, and I followed a few paces behind, trying to blend into the background so I wouldn't be noticed.

After walking down numerous corridors and up various flights of stairs, he came to a large, gilded door, which he knocked on. After the word "enter" was shouted, Leonardo went in the room and I slipped in behind him, hiding in the shadows.

It was a huge room, with a gilded, painted ceiling, and at one end of it was a black haired man with a beard sitting on a throne – Casare Borgia.

'I want you to create me a map of Imola. Do you think you can do it?' Borgia asked.

'Why yes, I am sure I can do that for you your Majesty.' Leonardo replied. He paused and then said, 'I don't like to mention it your Majesty, but funds are getting a little short and I have assistants and servants to pay.'

'Of course. See Machiavelli about that and I will instruct him to pay you', Borgia said.

'Thank you your Majesty.'

'You may go now, and return when you have completed the map. And take that cat with you too. I don't want animals in here, especially cats', Borgia said.

'But the smallest feline is a masterpiece your Majesty', Leonardo replied.

'To you perhaps, but not to me. Their fur irritates me.' At which point Borgia let out an earth shattering sneeze and Borgia's pet crow let out a long, hard squawk and shuffled its black feathers. It turned its beady eye on me and then swooped down towards me. Leonardo quickly opened the door and I ran out, with the crow following me, but Leonardo shooed it away and picked me up, running back down the stairs, holding me tightly in his arms.

We went back to Leonardo's rooms. As he opened the door, he jumped as he saw Machievelli sitting inside.

'How did you get in here?' Leonardo asked.

'I can get in anywhere' Machievelli replied. 'His Highness has instructed me to give you this' – he then dropped a large bag of coins onto the table.

'That was quick. I only mentioned I was short of money just now,' Leonardo said.

'His Highness thought you might need some money, so he had already instructed me to give it to you, before you just saw him,' Machievelli said.

Leonardo opened the bag and looked inside. 'Well, this should keep me going for a while.'

'I have also been instructed to give you this – a permit signed by His Majesty, which gives you entry to any area of his kingdom that you wish. You will need this to pass through the guards, especially when you are creating your map of Imola,' Machievelli said.

'Ah, so you know about that too,' said Leonardo.

'Of course, I know about everything. His Highness keeps me fully informed, and as his Special Advisor, he seeks my opinion on most things,' Machievelli said.

'I hear you are writing a book Machievelli', Leonardo said.

'Yes. It will be called The Prince. It will be the culmination of all my thoughts.' Machievelli replied.

'I think we disagree on most areas of your philosophy', Leonardo said.

'Yes', Machievelli said, 'I think so. My job is to present a positive spin on His Highness's actions. He agrees with me that it is far safer to be feared than loved if you cannot be both, and that inhuman cruelty is a virtue. Whilst it is important to give the appearance of being virtuous and truthful, a good ruler should be able to lie and act immorally when necessary. Fortune is a woman, and it is necessary, if one wants to hold her down, to beat her and strike her down. Brute force and deceit are necessary to be a good and effective ruler.'

Leonardo sighed when he listened to this, and turned away. 'Let us not argue Machievelli. I don't think we will ever agree on such things.'

'As you wish,' said Machievelli, as he swept out the door.

Now we were alone, and I could speak to him. An amazing thought – to be able to speak to a human being and be understood. Up until now, all I could do was meow, and most humans would guess from this that I wanted food – which most of the time was an accurate interpretation, but sometimes I wanted to say other things. Leonardo looked deeply into my eyes, picked me up and put me in his lap. He stroked my tabby fur and I purred.

'Well, it is a relief to be rid of him,' Leonardo said.

'My thoughts exactly,' I said. 'But you still haven't explained how you can understand what I'm saying – or how I got here.'

'It is a long story...' Leonardo began. The candlelight flickered in his eyes and his pale cheeks flushed. I licked the back of his hand to encourage him to continue. The smell of paint in the room made me feel a bit queasy, so I wanted him to hurry up and get on with it.

'You see I'm an old man now,' Leonardo said, 'But when I was younger I had such dreams and hopes. Now a lot of my dreams and hopes are dead. Vows begin when hope dies. I have so many regrets. I would give anything to go back in time so I could change the past and rectify my mistakes. I decided to create a box of regrets and try to transport it in a portal through time. I succeeded, so I then transported my cat through the portal in time too – and you are my cat. You forgot, because you have been forward and backwards in time.'

I sat wide eyed in amazement when I heard this. But it would explain why Leonardo had felt so familiar to me. I felt like I had known him before, in another life.

Leonardo continued: 'Regret crushes your heart – it does no good to dwell on past mistakes. We have to concentrate on the present moment because that is all that we have. We can't change the past and we don't know what the future will be. I had so much guilt about mistakes I had made in the past – times when I was cruel or stupid. Everyone has some darkness in their soul – a part of themselves they are ashamed of. We hate in others what we hate in ourselves, so if you meet someone you take an instant dislike to, it may be because they are a mirror for your own faults. It is important to forgive yourself and others for not being perfect. It's easier to forgive someone else than forgive yourself. I have to accept what I cannot change and change what I can. Rationally I knew that I couldn't change the past, but it didn't stop me wanting to travel through time, and at least try to rectify my mistakes.'

'But what do you feel guilty about?' I asked

'A long time ago, when I was much younger, I fell in love with another man. I do not feel guilt about that – I cannot see how love can be a crime, but unfortunately society does say it is a crime to love someone of the same sex. I foolishly let my affections show in public, and someone reported me to the authorities. They arrested me and put me in prison. No-one has the right to imprison another human being, whether man or animal, without due process. God gave to each the gift of freedom, and none can take it away. A lot of my so called friends deserted me and I was alone. I remember thinking in prison – 'I am without any friends...If there is no love – what then?' But I managed to endure prison, even though it nearly crushed me. I was constant like the phoenix, which understanding by its nature its renewal has the constancy to endure the burning flames which consume it, and then it is reborn anew.'

Leonardo put me on the floor and went to a large chest sitting in a corner of the room. He put his hand inside his shirt and pulled out a key which dangled from the end of a chain round his neck. He opened the large lock on the chest with the key. When Leonardo opened the lid a bright golden light suddenly shone out.

'This is the box of regrets', Leonardo said. 'But it is also the portal through time.' Rays of golden light filled the dark room until it was like a burning sun. I tried to move, but couldn't. I was frozen to the spot – mesmerised by the light.

Leonardo closed the lid on the box, picked me up and put me on his lap.

'I can't understand how all this can be possible', I said.

Leonardo sighed. 'It is very complicated. You may not understand it if I try to explain it to you, but I will try to keep it simple. You see there are really 10 dimensions – 6 invisible, and parallel universes. Everything is cyclical - the end of one thing is the beginning of something else and there is no beginning and no end. The universe is eternal – it has always existed – it always was and always will be. It started with a big bang, but it didn't come from nothing. The last universe died and collapsed into a black hole and from that black hole a new universe was formed. A black hole is born when a star dies – it is smaller than an atom but more massive than the sun. The same thing happens when people die - souls live on after death. It is with the greatest reluctance that the soul leaves the body, and I think that its sorrow and lamentations are not without cause. When someone dies their soul leaves their body and goes into another dimension and parallel universe where it's reincarnated. A neuron is a cell of the nervous system that conducts nerve impulses. There are neurons in the brain and the heart which are the same. Therefore the soul is in the heart.

Sometimes it's possible to enter the parallel universe through dreams or mirrors. Déjà vu can also be memories of the parallel universe or a past or future life. When people feel like they've met before their souls have usually met before in another life or a parallel universe. The universe and souls die and are reborn and reincarnated. We are all made from stardust. The stars are like Gods – they created us. The Earth and everything in it – including you and me, are all made from elements made in dying stars. Nebulae are clouds of particles and gases which contain remnants of dead stars - elements that create new stars and planets, and they also contain organic elements like amino acids, that were delivered to earth on meteorites. From these amino acids, life on earth began. The universe and the sun will die, but new stars are born from the death of old stars. When we die, the elements in our bodies go back to the universe and new souls are created. Everything is recycled, and everything is connected to everything else. There is a magic key that unlocks the door to the parallel universe, and that key is held on a chain around my neck - it opens that chest I just showed you.'

'But did you manage to change the past?' I asked.

'At first I found I couldn't change what had happened in the past, but I could erase its impact on the present.'

'How?' I asked.

'The mistakes I made in the past, which have led to my present predicament, in the parallel universes led to other outcomes. Anything is possible in another universe,' Leonardo replied.

'But how can you travel in time? I still don't understand?' I said.

'Through black holes. There aren't just big black holes in the universe, there are also miniature black holes. If you crammed enough matter together in the palm of your hand, you'd create a tiny black hole. If you look close enough you will see a world in a grain of sand and a heaven in a wild flower, hold Infinity in the palm of your hand and Eternity in an hour. A man called William Blake will write down those words I've just said in a few hundred years time. In the centre of our universe there is one huge black hole, which looks like an eye. The eye is the window of the soul. Another universe is right next door. It's hovering no more than a fraction of a millimetre away. If you time travel to the past, you can't change it. To change the past you need to travel not just through time but also from one parallel universe to another. That chest I showed you just now is a time machine. Inside it is a wormhole which leads to another wormhole in another universe. He turns not back who is bound to a star,' Leonardo said.

I tried to understand what Leonardo had told me, but my head was spinning.

'Does anyone else know all these things?' I asked.

'No,' Leonardo replied. 'You have to be very careful what you tell people. I keep all my ideas secret and I write my notes backwards and in code, so that you would need a mirror to read it and even then, it would be difficult. If the Pope and the Church found out what I know, I would be tortured and executed as a heretic. Anyone who challenges tradition and orthodoxy is considered mad or a heretic and is burnt at the stake. The Church does not want anyone upsetting its profitable status quo. Aristotle and the Bible said that the Earth is at the centre of the universe and all other planets – including the sun, revolve around it.

There is a Polish man called Copernicus who has said the sun is at the centre of the universe and all the planets, including the Earth, revolve around the sun. His theory will be proven in a hundred years by an Italian called Galileo Galilei, but he will be tried by the Inquisition, found "vehemently suspect of heresy", forced to recant, and spend the rest of his life under house arrest.

At the same time as Galileo there will be another great Italian called Giordano Bruno, and his ideas will be even more radical. Not only will he say the sun is at the centre of the universe, but also that the sun is a star. He will say the universe is infinite and it contains an infinite number of inhabited worlds populated by other intelligent beings. He will say: “The universe is then one, infinite, immobile.... It is not capable of comprehension and therefore is endless and limitless, and to that extent infinite and indeterminable, and consequently immobile.” He will also assert that the stars in the sky were really other suns like our own, around which orbited other planets. He will be tried by the Roman Inquisition, who will find him guilty of heresy and the great Catholic Church and Pope, in all its wisdom, will stick a metal spike in his tongue and burn him at the stake. That’s what happens when you tell the truth. No-one likes to hear the truth, especially the Pope.’

I jumped up onto the table and looked at Leonardo’s drawings. ‘What are these?’ I asked.

‘You won’t understand what these things are because they do not exist yet. With some I have tried to build a small model to test whether it works or not, but with others the technology doesn’t exist yet to build them. But they will be built in a few hundred years time. I will put the ideas in the heads of the inventors when they dream. There is a diving suit, helicopter, aeroplane, parachute, tank, telescope, missile, robot, car, contact lenses. There are also my medical drawings – my latest one shows hardening of the arteries – in a few hundred years they will call that Atherosclerosis. I have also just drawn the map His Highness Borgia requested – of the town of Imola,’ Leonardo said.

I looked at the map. It showed an aerial view of the town. ‘But how can you draw such a map? Surely only a bird has a view like that.’ I said.

‘Yes. I can become a bird and fly. Once you have tasted flight you will forever walk the world with your eyes turned skyward, for there you have been and there you will always long to return. I hate to see caged birds. Whenever I see the caged birds in the market place, I have to buy them and set them free,’ Leonardo said.

In a corner of the room was a painting of a beautiful, mysterious woman, with a strange half smile. ‘Who is that painting of?’ I asked.

‘Her name is Lisa Giconda. Her husband commissioned me to paint the picture many years ago in Florence, but I never finished it, so I have kept it and I keep working on it. Although I don't have her here as a model now so I have to use my assistant, Salai. He is quite feminine anyway, so I can use him as a model for men or women. I used him as a model for that painting over there of St John, and when I painted St John in the Last Supper mural in the monastery in Milan. The monks were not happy that St John looked like a woman, but I wasn't going to change it for them,' Leonardo said.

I walked over to the painting of the woman called Lisa, and stared into her eyes. Leonardo came over and placed a piece of paper vertically over one half of the painting and then over the other half.

'Do you see a difference in each half of the painting?' he asked.

'Yes. One half looks depressed, one half happy, one half is masculine and one half is feminine. The left eye turns inward, the right outward, the left corner of her mouth turns down, the right turns up,' I said.

'Yes, that's right. We contain opposites – happiness and sadness, masculinity and femininity. I know that many will say that this is a useless work, and these people will be those of whom Demetrius said that he took no more account of the wind from their mouths which caused these words, than of the wind which issued from their lower regions. These men possess a desire only for material wealth and are entirely devoid of the desire for wisdom, which is the sustenance and truly dependable wealth of the mind. I wanted to create a painting which would become immortal. Being able to travel through time gives me the ability to be slightly immortal, but eventually my body will die. When you give up your dreams, you die. My soul will live on though, as all souls are immortal. While I thought I was learning how to live, I've really been learning how to die. As a day well spent brings happy sleep, so a life well used brings contented death,' Leonardo said.

Leonardo showed me another drawing.

'You see this pattern I've designed here – of intertwining branches of vines and olives. I painted this recently on the walls and ceilings of His Highness's palace, but I've painted the same design in an Egyptian tomb which dates to 1500BC. Ancient Egypt is an amazing place. You would like it there, as they worship cats as Gods, but unfortunately they also kill a lot of cats as a gift to the Gods. In the temples there are thousands of mummified cats. Quite horrifying,' Leonardo said.

I shuddered. 'Where did you learn how to do all this?' I asked.

'I have taught myself everything I know. I cannot quote from eminent authors…I do know that all knowledge is vain and full of error when it is not born of experience. And so experience will be my mistress. All our knowledge proceeds from what we feel. Nature is the source of all true knowledge. Look around you and you will see art in everything. It should not be hard for you to stop sometimes and look into the stains of walls, or ashes of a fire, or clouds, or mud or like places, in which you may find really marvellous ideas. If you study anything in great detail, as I do, it will be hard not to fall in love with it, as great love is born of thorough knowledge of the beloved.

I have a reputation for never finishing anything, but art is never finished, only abandoned. Sometimes I wonder if I have I done anything of worth. I argued recently with Michelangelo, who is so convinced sculpture is superior to painting. I said to him "Don't pity the humble painter. He can be Lord of all things. Whatever exists in the universe he has first in his mind and then in his hand. By his art he may be called the grandchild of God,"' Leonardo said.

Leonardo stood up and stretched. 'Of course I am getting old now, and ill. Try to keep in good health, you will do so better if you avoid doctors, for their drugs are a kind of alchemy, which has produced many books as remedies. People choose as healers persons who understand nothing about the illnesses they treat. Dr's are destroyers of lives. Dr's created me and destroyed me. Medicine is the restoration of elements out of equilibrium; illness is the discord of elements infused into the living body. Iron rusts when it is not used, stagnant water loses its purity and freezes over when cold; so, too, does inactivity sap the vigour of the mind. So it is important to try and stay active in mind and body,' Leonardo said.

Suddenly the earth shook. Leonardo rushed over to the chest in the corner – the portal through time. He quickly unlocked the chest, picked me up and jumped inside, closing the lid just as the ceiling came crashing down.

CHAPTER 6

London, England, 2050

When Leonardo opened the lid of the chest and we climbed out, we were in a dark alley. It was freezing cold and windy. At first I thought we might have landed in Siberia.

'Where are we?' I asked.

'This is London, England, in the year 2050. Not somewhere I intended to go, but in a rush you have to pull in wherever you can. This is not a nice place, so we will have to be very careful,' Leonardo said.

'What's wrong with it?' I asked.

'This is the culmination of Machievelli and Borgia's philosophy – a place where the Government is brutal and cruel, where the poor and disabled are put in workhouses and concentration camps,' Leonardo said.

'And the people accept this?' I asked.

'Yes, because the Government use the same tactic as the Nazis did in 1930s Germany – they used propaganda in the newspapers to breed hatred against the Jews by portraying them as vermin. This current Government use the same tactic – they use propaganda in the newspapers to portray the poor and disabled as vermin too. So the general population attack the poor and disabled in the street, and they are quite happy that the Government have put them in concentration camps and workhouses. The Government don't call them concentration camps and workhouses though – they call the workhouses "Workfare" and the concentration camps are NHS Hospitals where the murder is called the "Liverpool Care Pathway". These Hospitals are given money according to how many people they kill, so the more poor people they murder, the more money the Government gives them.

The Government long ago scrapped Human Rights Law, the Welfare State and privatised the NHS. They scrapped welfare benefits, Legal Aid, free healthcare. The Government are the opposite of Robin Hood – he stole from the rich and gave to the poor, but this Government steal from the poor and give to the rich. The money the Government have stolen from the poor by scrapping benefits, Legal Aid and free healthcare, is used to pay for tax cuts for the rich. The rich and powerful tell the Government what policies they want and they pay the Government to introduce these policies. It is a brutal, cruel, corrupt Government. Their policy is to make the rich and powerful richer and more powerful and the poor and powerless poorer and more powerless. There are two other political parties, but they just agree with all of the Governments policies, so there is no real opposition.

There is no-one to stand up for the poor, powerless and oppressed. There is no equality or justice. Only the rich have access to healthcare and legal help. The rich and powerful can get away with any crime they like – rape, murder, fraud, yet the poor and powerless get sent to prison for the slightest little thing. The Government need a scapegoat – someone to blame for the recession, so they blame the poor and disabled, in the same way the Nazis blamed the Jews in the 1930s. The poor and disabled are murdered – like the Nazis exterminated the Jews. First they are sent to the workhouses, but if they refuse to go there, they are sent to the concentration camps, although if they get too sick or ill they are sent to the concentration camps anyway.

The Prime Minister here is called Simon Orifice.' Leonardo pointed to a poster showing a man with a fat, round face, and a smug, conceited smile. 'The only job requirement to work in the Government or Council is to be incompetent, rude, corrupt, vicious. Their motto is: "Nothing ever gets done, or gets done well." People who work in the Government or Council used to be called Civil Servants but now they are called Mega Morons. The Religious order here is called the Paedophile Church, and the Head of it is Paedophile in Chief. They are against homosexuality, abortion and contraception, but paedophilia and child abuse is compulsory,' Leonardo said.

In the alley a woman rose up from under a pile of cardboard boxes. She was in her late 60s, very thin, dressed in dirty rags, with matted brown hair, bloodshot eyes and a face lined and pale. Her sunken cheeks highlighted the bones in her skull. She raised her eyes towards us and rubbed her wide jaw, which was bleeding. She shuffled towards us.

'Do you have any food?' She asked.

'No, I am sorry, we don't,' Leonardo replied. 'What's your name?'

'Louise', she said.

Louise was my previous owner, but surely it couldn't be the same woman. I thought she was dead. I stared at her, and suddenly I realised it WAS the same woman. I hardly recognised her - she looked so much older and more haggard. I walked up to her and rubbed against her ankles. She bent down and stroked me.

'I used to have a cat like you once, a long time ago. You look so much like him, but you can't be the same cat, as I had him 30 years ago, and he would be dead by now,' Louise said.

I longed to tell Louise that I WAS the same cat she had 30 years ago, but she couldn't understand the cat language. The only human I'd met who could understand cat was Leonardo.

Louise looked into Leonardo's eyes and said, 'I can't remember the last time I laughed long and hard, felt love and hope, or the last time I had a good eight hours sleep. I haven't done any of those things for years, and maybe I'll never do any of them again. This Government is oppressing not just me, but everyone who is poor, weak, disabled, powerless, working-class. It's a game where all the odds are stacked against me and I haven't been told what the rules are. Some people give up and kill themselves, but I'm not going to give this Government the satisfaction of killing me or breaking my will or spirit. They want to do that, but I'm not going to give them the satisfaction. They can put me in prison, take away all my money and my home. And along the way some people will cut off contact with me – the small minded, judgmental people. But my true friends will stick by me. The Government can't take away my mind, soul, spirit. They can try and break me and destroy me, but I won't let them succeed. It's impossible to win against this Government – they're all powerful, and they're evil, corrupt Fascists. They've made sure the poor can't vote, but all the parties are the same now anyway. I am trying to organise a resistance movement. This is one of my posters.' Louise handed Leonardo a piece of paper which said: "Freedom is in peril. Defend it with all your might.' She started to cough. Her hand reached out to the wall to prop herself up.

'My father died recently,' she continued, 'and the strangest thing is that there is a gravestone in front of his which has the same name on it, but this other person died in 1900 age 16. On the gravestone it says "out of weakness we're made strong". My Mum died 4 years ago. A few months after she died, I was lying in bed and all of her things fell over in the next room. I went out on the landing and I felt like she was standing there, although I couldn't see her. But I could smell her and feel her. You probably think I'm crazy,' Louise said.

'No, not at all.' Leonardo replied. 'You are right about this Government and things will just get worse here if you stay. As for your father, the gravestone you mentioned with his name on is a blip from a parallel universe. Same name, same soul, different date. Your mother's soul came back to visit you after she died, that's why you felt her presence. We are all connected and everything happens for a reason – as you will find out.'

'Now I'm starting to think you're the one who's crazy.' Louise said.

'There's a thin line between sanity and insanity. It is usually the outsiders or freethinkers who are considered insane,' Leonardo replied.

'I have so many regrets', Louse said. 'I had the chance to go to Cambridge University when I was younger, but I didn't even apply. My life might have been different if I had gone – maybe I would have been a success instead of a failure. I've always had a dream of being a writer, but I've tried writing novels and no-one is interested. I don't know which is worse – trying to fulfil your dreams and failing, or never trying at all. I realise now that I have all the qualities I hate in other people. I treated my mother badly. I never helped her, appreciated or valued her until she died, and it was too late then. I feel like I killed her with my selfishness. My parents did everything for me but I did nothing for them. I took them for granted. It is only when you lose someone forever that you realise what you've lost. The guilt I feel is torturing me. I've created a prison of my own making – full of guilt, regrets, shame. I'm punishing myself. The past is weighing me down – all the guilt and regrets are like a huge lump of lead, pressing down on my heart and soul.'

'I know all about guilt and regrets. They are a heavy burden,' Leonardo said. 'Forgiveness will set you free. Everyone makes mistakes - no-one is perfect. It is easier to forgive others than to forgive yourself. Self punishment serves no useful purpose. Nothing positive can come from blaming yourself. You have to accept what you can't change, and you can't change the past. Just because you have faults and made mistakes doesn't make you a bad person. Everyone is a mixture of good and bad. In law it is the intention to malice that counts. Murder is premeditated, planned, and with the intention to kill. Manslaughter is without malice aforethought - without the intention to kill. Your intention was not to kill your mother, hurt her, make her suffer and be unhappy – was it?'

'No, of course not,' Louise replied.

'You can't blame yourself for not being able to see into the future and see the consequences of your actions. You are blaming yourself for being human, because no ordinary human can see into the future. We all make decisions based on what we know of the past and present. The past is weighing you down. You have to free yourself from it. Blaming yourself won't achieve anything. All your guilt and regrets won't bring your parents back and it won't change the past. You need serenity to accept the things you cannot change, courage to change the things you can, and the wisdom to know the difference.

We are all powerless to control the past. Even if you'd done all the things you wished you'd done, the outcome may have been the same, and your mother may still have died. Your mother wouldn't want you to suffer, be unhappy, blame yourself. Your mother would forgive you, so forgive yourself for not being perfect – for being human. As long as you let the guilt and regrets weigh you down, you will be forever chained to the past. Once you let it go, you will be free to head into the future. The past is gone forever. All you have is the present – that is the only thing you can change. There is no point making the present a living hell full of guilt and regrets. You have created this prison, so you have the key to set yourself free, and the key is forgiveness.

Your guilt and shame is your conscience telling you what you did was wrong. It shows you do care about your mother. If you didn't care, you wouldn't feel guilt. You have to forgive the person you were then and the person you are now. We experience great unhappiness for a reason – to make us stronger or to learn something. Sometimes we get what we need instead of what we want. The most important thing is to feel a connection with someone or something, to know yourself and to have nothing in excess. If you don't know where you're going, it doesn't matter which path you take. Though no one can go back and make a brand new start, anyone can start from now and make a brand new end. Don't give up. You decide your own fate,' Leonardo replied.

I wrapped myself around Louise's legs. She picked me up and held me tightly. Tears were streaming down her face. I licked them, rubbed the side of my face against hers and purred. I put the soft, warm pad of my paw against her cheek and looked into her eyes.

'Oh Tom. You are still my best friend,' Louise said.

Out of the corner of my eye, I saw a mouse scurrying around. I jumped down from Louise's arms, chased the mouse and caught it, but instead of just giving up and letting me eat it – as most mice do, or struggling and just making things worse (for the mouse rather than me), this one started to engage me in conversation:-

'I am the leader of the Trade Union and Political Party called the Mouse Party,' the mouse stated, in a very agitated way, 'and I demand full legal representation regarding your attempt to eat me.'

I was a bit taken aback by this, but I thought I would humour him.

'Well, bring on your lawyer then,' I said, in contempt.

The mouse let out a long, hard squeak (quite deafening for such a small creature), and out of the shadows a meerkat appeared.

'I am Jerry the Meerkat – top lawyer and world record scorpion catcher.' He held out his card.

'You look familiar. Have I seen you before?' I asked.

'You are confusing me with my cousin, who is a film star. We look very similar. I could have been a film star myself of course, but he had a good agent, who got him some good parts. I personally think Sea Otters could become the next Big Thing, the next Big Meerkat, if they could just get the same publicity and PR agent. In fact I was considering becoming an agent myself and offering my services to the Sea Otters,' Jerry said.

The mouse suddenly shouted: 'Jerry, PLEASE….can we just concentrate on the facts here – like the fact that I'm about to be eaten.'

At this point Leonardo came over, to see what was happening.

'Ahhh…Jerry, we meet again,' Leonard said.

Jerry bowed. 'It is an honour to be in your presence again,' Jerry replied.

I was confused by this. 'How can you have met before?' I asked.

'Jerry popped up in one of my travels', Leonardo replied. 'He is a good lawyer. Although when it comes to the real heroes of the animal kingdom, no-one can match the whales and dolphins. Humpback whales protect seals from attacks by killer whales and dolphins protect people from shark attack. What other animal would protect a totally different species? And they are both so intelligent. When souls are reincarnated, only the most intelligent become whales and dolphins, and cats of course.'

Louise came over and looked in amazement at us all. 'How come you can talk to animals?' She asked Leonardo.

'It is a gift I have', he replied.

'Well, it must be nice to have that ability. It would be even nicer if you could get me out of this hell hole,' she said.

'I will try to help you if I can. If your life is miserable then you must do everything you can to fight to change it. Don't just give up without a fight. Only accept what you cannot change. We're prisoners of our imagination and sometimes what we fear is just inside our heads and not a reality, but in your case I know it is a reality. This world is evil and dangerous. But the word "crisis" comes from the Greek word meaning "passage", so we will find a way out of this crisis,' Leonardo said.

Suddenly a policeman appeared at the entrance to the alley we were standing in. He carried a large machine gun, which he pointed at us.

'What are you doing here?' He shouted.

'Nothing. Just talking.' Louise replied.

The policeman came over to Louise and held the gun under her chin.

'ID', he shouted.

Louise pulled out an ID card from her pocket and showed it to him. He looked at it, handed it back to her, and then turned to Leonardo. 'ID', he shouted.

'I do not have any I'm afraid, as I have just arrived in your country,' Leonardo said.

'Immigrant without ID,' the policeman barked into his walkie talkie.

'You will have to come down to the police station.' The policeman grabbed hold of Leonardo's arm and pulled him towards the entrance of the alley. Leonardo struggled. The policeman hit Leonardo over the head with the butt of his gun, and Leonardo fell to the floor.

'Please don't hurt him,' Louise said. 'He has applied for his ID, but it hasn't come through yet.'

The policeman hit Louise over the head with the butt of his gun and she fell to the floor too.

I bit the policeman's ankle. He let out a cry and fired his gun at me, but missed. I then jumped up and bit him on the hand and he dropped his gun.

Leonardo and Louise started to come round, and Leonardo quickly picked up the gun before the policeman could. He aimed it at the policeman.

'Go,' Leonardo said, and the policeman ran off.

'I know a place we can hide,' Louise said, and she pulled Leonardo through a door in the alley and I followed.

We were inside a large factory. People sat in rows, putting things on conveyor belts.

'This is the workhouse,' Louise whispered. 'This is where I'm supposed to live, but I ran away.'

"Work sets you free" was written in large letters on the wall.

Louise pointed at the slogan and said to Leonardo: 'See what that says. Those words were written at the entrance to a Nazi concentration camp in Germany in the 1930s, and the present Government has adopted it as its slogan too. They haven't just put it in the workhouses, but they've put it at the entrance to the present day concentration camps too. If you are poor, sick or disabled you are sent to the workhouse first, and if you become too sick to work there, or you rebel and refuse to work or run away, they send you to the concentration camps, where you are murdered. If they find me, I will be sent to the concentration camp too, so we can't stay here for long. I know a way out of here though.'

'It would be best if we can escape to the countryside, as we are less likely to be found there,' Leonardo said.

'There is no countryside anymore. Construction firms paid the Government years ago to scrap all planning laws, so the law saying you can't build on green belt land was scrapped, and then private houses were built for the middle and upper classes. The Government scrapped council housing years ago too, and forced the poor out of their homes, so they either had to sleep on the streets or go in the workhouse.'

'Where can we hide then?' Leonardo asked.

'There aren't many places. There are cameras everywhere, watching everyone. The Government spy on people's emails, phone calls, the websites they visit. They have undercover spies watching and filming people too. Anyone they class as subversive, they put on an Extremism Database, and they assign their own personal spy, to follow them and film them. I managed to give mine the slip, and I know where most of the cameras are around here, so I can avoid them. They're very small but I can spot them most of the time, although some I miss. Follow me,' Louise whispered, as she led Leonardo and me through a small passageway. It was very dark and full of cobwebs and spiders.

As we were half way down the narrow passage, a loud male voice shouted at us to stop. We all started running as fast as we could, but only Louise knew where we going. We got to the end of the passage and Louise flung open a door. We all ran right through, but we no longer had our feet on the ground – we were falling through the air. It was still dark, so it was like falling down a hole into a long tunnel.

Cats are the greatest at falling of course. We can turn our bodies round so we land on our feet. The best way to fall is to relax, stretch out, smoke a pipe, enjoy the passing scenery, until your paws land on the ground.

We kept falling for a long time, until I didn't think we would ever stop. The tunnel narrowed and squeezed us until I could hardly breathe. Then I lost consciousness.

CHAPTER 7

Egypt, 1332 BC

When I opened my eyes, we were in a dark, underground tomb. Leonardo and Louise were lying next to me on the floor, and they started to come round too.

A man came into the tomb, with a shaved head and only wearing a white linen loincloth. He carried a candle, which he put down on the floor. He couldn't see us as we were in a dark corner the light didn't reach. He started to paint on the wall – a picture of a tabby cat, which looked remarkably like me, hunting in the marshes. The cat was leaping in the air, and had caught three birds, which it grasped between its front and back paws, and its mouth. Also in the marshes with the cat were a man, woman and child on a boat. The man was hunting birds too, and had a boomerang in his hand. I presume they were the cat's owners. The artist was painting the detail of the cat's fur very well, and the picture was very life like.

Eventually he went out of the tomb, and we quickly followed him. When we came out of the tomb the sunlight almost blinded me. It was so hot the sand burnt my paws.

'Where are we?' Louise asked.

'Egypt, in 1332 BC.' Leonardo replied.

'How did we get here?' Louise asked.

'We fell down a wormhole through space and time,' Leonardo replied.

'What?' Louise said.

'It would take too long to explain now. We need to seek shelter,' Leonardo said.

Leonardo started walking quickly like he knew where he was going, so Louise and I followed him.

Eventually we came to a temple. Outside the temple were large statues of cats – a good sign. We went in and Leonardo started talking to one of the priests:

'I would like to make an offering to the goddess Bastet,' Leonardo said.

The priest was a small fat man, with a shaved head and a large stomach overhanging the waist of his loincloth. The priest sighed.

'We have three price ranges,' the priest said, in a bored monotone. 'Your basic cheap package consists of a whisker or scrap of fur, wrapped in bandages in the shape of a cat. Our middle range package consists of bits of various different animals, wrapped in bandages in the shape of the cat. Or, we have our deluxe, top of the range, actual, real, whole cat, genuinely mummified and realistically painted. You pays your money, you takes your choice.'

'I will have your deluxe package. How much is it?' Leonardo asked.

The priest gave Leonardo a withering look.

'I don't think you would be able to afford it,' the priest said as he looked at Leonardo's shabby, dirty, torn robes.

Leonardo reached into his pocket and pulled out a gold coin.

'Would this be enough?' Leonardo asked, as he handed the coin to the priest. The priest raised his eyebrows in surprise.

'That will do nicely,' he said, as he took the coin from Leonardo.

The priest handed Leonardo a mummified cat.

'You will have to hurry as the King is due here any minute,' the priest said.

'And that would be Tutankhamun?' Leonardo asked.

'Of course. There is only one king.' The priest replied.

Leonardo went into a courtyard inside the temple and placed the mummified cat against a wall, whilst saying: 'An offering to you oh mighty Bastet, great cat goddess and guardian angel.' He bowed.

Louise stayed at the entrance to the temple, talking to the priest, but I followed Leonardo, intrigued. While he was making his offering, I weaved in and out of his legs, purring and rubbing the side of my face against his ankles. He bent down and started stroking me. I wrapped myself around his ankles even more tightly, especially when he stroked me under the chin and the side of my face. Ah, there's nothing like a really good stroking!

Leonardo picked me up and held me in his arms. I put a paw on his shoulder, looked him in the eyes and said: 'What is all this stuff about Bastet?'

'Bastet is the great Egyptian cat goddess. Unfortunately in order to worship her, priests kill cats, mummify them and people pay to give them as offerings, which I can't quite understand, but that's priests for you – always on the look out to make easy money,' Leonardo said.

'Worshiping cats sounds very sensible. The Egyptians must be a very intelligent race of people,' I said.

'Oh they are,' Leonardo replied. 'Their art is wonderful, although most of it is hidden away in tombs, temples and the Kings palace so not many people see it. '

Louise got bored talking to the Priest, so she joined us inside the temple. Leonardo pointed to the brightly coloured paintings on the walls and columns and said to her: 'The Egyptians believe that to speak the name of the dead makes them live again. They write letters to the dead as they believe the dead can help the living. They think the dead pass into another sphere of existence, where their heart is weighed and if they have an evil, heavy heart it will be fed to a monster that will devour and destroy it. If their heart is light and good, they are allowed to pass into the afterlife, where they live forever in paradise.'

The smell of incense wafted through the temple and we all fell into a trance, where the souls of the dead could almost touch us and speak to us.

Suddenly a trumpet made a very loud noise which went right through me and made my fur stand on end. A man walked into the courtyard wearing many jewels and a golden crown. The King Tutankhamun had arrived.

Tutankhamun was carrying a mummified cat, which he placed next to Leonardo's offering. Leonardo bowed as the King approached.

'A nice cat you have there,Tutankhamun said, and he proceeded to stroke me. 'I have a cat myself in the palace. You are dressed very strangely. Are you a foreigner?'

'Yes your Majesty. I have not had time to buy the right clothes,' Leonardo replied.

'What is your occupation?' Tutankhamun asked.

'I am an artist and inventor,' replied Leonardo.

'Ah, well that's interesting, and a fortunate co-incidence, because I have been looking for a good artist and inventor to redecorate the palace and install some modern conveniences. I hear that in Pakistan and India they have plumbing, with flushing toilets, if you can believe such a thing,' Tutankhamun said.

'Oh yes that is true your Highness, and I could quite easily install such a system in your own palace, if you would be gracious enough to employ me.' Leonardo bowed.

'Well that's settled then. You will work for me and I will provide you with all food and lodgings, as well as payment of course. And please bring your cat too, as my cat seems quite lonely and bored at the moment – I think she needs a companion, and who knows, maybe a romance will follow and we might hear the pitter patter of tiny paws.' Tutankhamun laughed and stroked me.

Sounded like a good idea to me. I hate blind dates, but the King's cat sounded like a hot prospect – one I couldn't refuse. I couldn't remember the last time I had some good fur on fur action.

'Just one thing your Highness. Would it be possible for my friend here to join us?' Leonardo pointed to Louise. 'I am sure she would be able to be a helpful assistant to me in my work.'

'Oh yes, of course, bring her along. Although she is dressed very strangely too. But we can provide you and your friend with appropriate clothes,' Tutankhamun replied.

We all then got into the King's chariot – which was a bit of a tight squeeze, and headed off towards the palace.

When we finally arrived I was stunned by the vastness of it – huge pillars, painted with brightly coloured figures, and in the Kings quarters, beautiful gilded furniture, decorated with pictures inlaid with gemstones and enamel. Everything sparkled – with gold, rubies, sapphires, emeralds.

But what really stunned me was the Kings cat – who was sitting next to his golden throne. It was Crystal – the white cat I knew before, with the odd coloured eyes and delusions of being human. I went up to her and said: 'Do you remember me?'

'No,' she replied.

'We've met before, in another time and place,' I said.

'Well I can't remember it.' Crystal replied. She turned up her nose at me in the most snooty fashion, and flounced off.

'Well so much for a dream romance,' I thought to myself. But I could easily find another cat somewhere else, so it didn't bother me. Although I was irritated by her superior attitude – as if she was better than me, just because she was the King's cat. Perhaps I should teach her a lesson – make her fall in love with me and then dump her. Hah – yes, the perfect plan!

I saw Leonardo walking through one of the huge, long corridors, talking to Louise, so I followed him and they went into a room, which had a bed, so I assumed this would be our new home.

'I don't know how I can be your assistant, I don't know how to draw or paint,' Louise said.

'I will teach you. I usually have boy apprentices, but you can be my first female apprentice. Plus this will be a good opportunity for you to start again, with a completely new life. The world is your oyster,' Leonardo said.

'Or my cesspit. I'm not what you would call an optimist. When the world has constantly kicked you in the teeth all your life, it's hard to think things will ever be any different.' Louise sighed. Her hunched shoulders slumped into a depressed, dispirited slouch.

'You must have hope,' Leonardo said. 'Without hope it is hard to carry on. You end up just existing rather than living.'

'I used to have hope, but every dream or ambition I had has died. There are only so many dead ends you can go down, and so many failures, rejections and defeats you can cope with before you just give up,' Louise said.

'I know that feeling well. I have felt like a failure myself so many times. I have a reputation for never finishing anything, but when you are a perfectionist it is hard to think anything is perfect enough to finish,' Leonardo said.

Leonardo tenderly put his hand on Louise's shoulder and said: 'Come over here.' He guided her to a table and put a piece of paper and pencil in front of her. 'I will teach you to draw, and then you will realise there is something you can do well,' he said.

Leonardo drew a picture of me on the paper and handed it to Louise. 'Now see if you can copy that,' he said.

Louise tried and gave the paper back to him.

'It is no good,' she said. 'It looks more like a rabbit than a cat.'

'Don't give up so easily. You can't expect to draw straight away. I will teach you, but it will take a long time. You have to be patient,' Leonardo said.

A man suddenly appeared at the door and said: 'His highness wishes to speak to you.'

Leonardo followed him down the maze of corridors, and entered Tutankhamun's private quarters. I was close behind, blending into the shadows so as not to be seen.

'I have a challenge for you,' Tutankhamun said.

Leonardo bowed. 'Whatever you desire your highness, I will try to fulfil.'

'I think someone is planning to murder me. Do you think you can stop him?' Tutankhamun said.

'Do you know who?' Leonardo asked.

'It is my General. He thinks I don't suspect, but I have my spies. I know I hired you as an artist and inventor rather than as a bodyguard, but I thought you might have some ideas about how to prevent an attack,' Tutankhamun said.

'I will think about it your highness, and will try to come up with a plan. I will need to study this man, to try and investigate his methods. Could you point him out to me?' Leonardo asked.

'Follow me.' Tutankhamun said. He led Leonardo to a balcony. Down below was a large courtyard, full of soldiers.

'There is the General', Tutankhamun said.

The General was a large, fat man with a bald head and big nose, sitting on a horse, barking orders to his men.

'He does not seem a pleasant type,' Leonardo remarked.

'He would give anything to see me dead, so he can become Pharaoh himself,' Tutankhamun replied.

'Let me investigate and I will try to construct a plan your highness. But why do you just not arrest him?' Leonardo asked.

'He has the whole army under his command. If I ordered his arrest, I do not know whether the army would be loyal to me or to him. He could order the army to overthrow me and take command. I don't want him to suspect that I know what his plans are. I want to take him by surprise, and dispose of him in a discrete way,' Tutankhamun replied.

'Do you mean you would like him assassinated?' Leonardo asked.

'If that is the only way of getting rid of him, then yes. It is my life against his. Plus he also has designs on my wife. She has told me he has made advances to her. If he murders me, he will force her to marry him, in order to legitimise his rule. She has told me that if such a thing happens, she would write to the King of our former enemy, in a neighbouring country, and ask him to send one of his sons for her to marry, as she would rather marry him than marry the General. I will reward you richly if you can complete this task. Usually you have to complete 3 tasks in order to win one prize, but in this case, if you complete this one task, I will give you 3 wishes,' Tutankhamun said.

After this conversation, Leonardo studied the General, followed him, made notes and plans.

I also made my own study – of Tutankhamun's cat Crystal. I decided to act aloof and cool with her. No cat likes to be ignored, especially a female cat, and I could see I was getting to Crystal. The cold shoulder was working, until it got to the stage where she walked right up to me and swiped my face with her paw.

'What was that for?' I said, trying to hide my pain.

'You are the rudest cat I have ever met,' she replied.

'Well you were ruder to me, so I decided to give you a taste of your own medicine,' I replied.

'It's not my fault I can't remember you. I think you must be crazy to think we met in a former life,' Crystal said.

'Well, it's true,' I said.

'So you can travel through time?' She said in a mocking tone.

'Yes,' I said.

'Well prove it.' She said.

'OK. Follow me'. And I walked to our room, where I pointed to Leonardo's notes and drawings, and the chest in the corner.

'Leonardo has a magic key around his neck, and with that key he can unlock that chest over there and we can travel through time. Don't ask me how it's done, because I don't understand it. If you look at his notes and drawings you will see things that won't be invented for thousands of years,' I said.

'How am I supposed to know they will ever be invented?' She asked. 'Leonardo must be just as mad as you are. And how can you carry a chest through time?' And with that she tried to flounce out the room, but I barred her way, by lodging myself in the entrance to the door.

'I know it is hard to believe and I don't know how I can prove it to you. I don't know how the chest travels through time with us, but it does – it is always just there, whenever we need it.' I sighed and said: 'But even if you don't remember the first time we met, can't you at least give me a chance, and try to like me a little bit?' I looked at her with my most appealing eyes, and touched my nose against hers. Her face softened and she smiled.

'I suppose I could give you a chance,' she said.

I rubbed my face against the side of hers and we both started to purr. At last I was getting somewhere! I was feeling quite amorous, and was just about to start strenuous sexual proceedings, when Leonardo burst into the room and nearly fell over me.

'Oh Tom, what are doing blocking the door?' He asked.

I looked at Crystal and he quickly assessed the situation correctly.

'Ah, I see you are in courtship proceedings,' Leonardo said.

'You assume correctly,' I replied.

'Leonardo can understand what you say – he can understand cat! That's impossible,' said Crystal.

'It is not impossible,' said Leonardo.

Crystal was stunned into silence. When she finally recovered, she said to Leonardo: 'Tom tells me you can travel through time, but why would you want to do such a thing?'

'I wanted to travel though time to try and rectify mistakes I'd made in the past, which made me feel a great deal of guilt,' Leonardo said.

'But why do you feel guilty?' Crystal asked.

'I swallowed a poison labelled "guilt, mistakes, regrets, imperfection." The antidote to this, which is needed to purge the poison from my body is a medicine labelled "love, forgiveness, acceptance." This is the medicine I am trying to seek. Guilt is a horrible thing. It is like a heavy weight crushing my heart. The poison is eating away at my soul. I must seek redemption.' Leonardo sighed and sat down.

Suddenly the door burst open and Louise ran into the room: 'Come quickly, Tutankhamun has been killed,' She shouted.

We all ran after her until we came to Tutankhamun's private quarters. He was lying in bed, with a Doctor standing over him.

'What has happened?' Leonardo asked the Doctor.

'I am not sure. The General told me His Highness had an accident while hunting, and fell from his carriage, but it looks to me like His Highness has been hit over the head. I suppose the General could be right, after all, why would he lie about such a thing?' The Doctor said.

Leonardo looked at me – we both knew the answer to that.

'Is he dead?' Leonardo asked the Doctor.

'He was alive when I first saw him, but only for a brief moment. Now he is dead.' The Doctor said.

'Did he manage to say anything before he died?' asked Leonardo.

'Yes. He said "Leonardo will know". Strange thing to say – do you know what he meant?' the Doctor asked.

'Yes. I know what he meant. It is vital I see Tutankhamun's wife as soon as possible.' Leonardo said. 'Where is she?'

'I don't know,' the Doctor replied.

'Where is the General then?' Leonardo asked.

'I don't know that either I am afraid, but I will try to find him and the Queen.' The Doctor rushed out of the room and we were alone.

Leonardo looked at Tutankhamun's body and whispered: 'I am sorry. I was too late to save you.' He held Tutankhamun's hand in his and kissed it. Tears fell from Leonardo's eyes and he breathed a heavy sigh.

I rubbed the side of my face against Leonardo's ankles. He bent down and picked me up. I licked away the tears that were running down his cheeks. Leonardo hugged me closely to him and kissed the top of my head.

'You are a good cat Tom. I know you are trying to comfort me. It is too dangerous for us to stay here now. We have to leave,' Leonardo said.

Still carrying me in his arms, we all ran back to Leonardo's room. In the corner was the chest. Leonardo opened it with his magic key and the room was filled with a golden light.

Louise picked up Crystal and said: 'Can we come too?'

'Of course. Jump in,' Leonardo said.

Leonardo jumped into the chest, still holding me in his arms, and Louise followed us, carrying Crystal in her arms.

CHAPTER 8

Greece, 530BC

Before I could twitch my whiskers we'd landed in another very hot, sunny country, with men walking around in togas.

'Where are we now?' Louise asked.

'A Greek island off the coast of Turkey, called Samos. It is 530BC and I need to find a man called Pythagoras. I've got to catch him before he gets on a boat,' Leonardo replied.

We were standing on the coast, in a small harbour, with a wooden pier jutting out into the azure sea. A middle aged man with a long white beard was getting onto a boat. Leonardo ran towards him and we all followed. By the time we arrived, we were all out of breath and panting, especially Leonardo, who had sweat running down his face. We reached the boat just in time before it set sail.

Leonardo went up to Pythagoras and shook his hand.

'It is a great honour to meet you,' Leonardo said.

Pythagoras looked puzzled.

'I'm sorry, but I cannot recall ever having met you before,' Pythagoras replied.

'We haven't met before, but I know of your great reputation,' Leonardo said. 'I hear that you are going to set up a religious sect and I would like to join you.'

'You are welcome to join my group, but first I would like to know more about you. I would like to make sure you agree with the principles of my group,' Pythagoras said.

'I think we have a lot in common,' Leonardo replied. 'We are both vegetarians, we both believe that the soul leaves the body after death and is reincarnated. I am not sure about numerology though – your belief that numbers rule the universe and they are magical. I think you are probably right about that, but I would like to know more before I decide for certain.'

'Of course. It is right to be sceptical about everything and not believe things without evidence and proof,'

Pythagoras replied. 'I learnt everything I know from three great teachers – a priestess at Delphi called Themistoclea , an Egyptian priest, and Pherecydes of Syros. As for reincarnation, I was telling this story to a pupil of mine called Plato, who said he would put it in a book he is writing called the Republic. The story is that Er, the son of Armenius, miraculously returned to life on the twelfth day after death and recounted the secrets of the other world. After death, he said, he went with others to the place of Judgment and saw the souls returning from heaven, and proceeded with them to a place where they chose new lives, human and animal. Men were seen passing into animals and wild and tame animals changing into each other. After their choice the souls drank of Lethe – the river of forgetfulness, and then shot away like stars to their re-birth.

The number of souls is fixed; birth therefore is never the creation of a soul, but only a transmigration from one body to another. The soul reincarnates again and again into the bodies of humans, animals, or vegetables until it becomes immortal. The other day I stopped a man who was beating a dog, as I recognised in its cries the voice of a departed friend. I know who I have been in previous lives - Euphorbus the son of Panthus, in the Trojan War, as well as a tradesman and a courtesan.'

'I believe we also share something else,' Leonardo said, 'the ability to travel through space and time, and to communicate with animals and plants.'

Pythagoras looked stunned.

'I have never disclosed my skills in that area to anyone, and I didn't think anyone on earth possessed a similar ability,' Pythagoras said.

Pythagoras and Leonardo spent many hours talking on the boat. Pythagoras again mentioned his pupil Plato:

'I was telling another story to Plato, which he said he would also put in this book he is writing called The Republic. The story is that Glaucon, taking up Thrasymachus' challenge, recounts a myth of the magical ring of Gyges. According to the myth, Gyges becomes king of Lydia when he stumbles upon a magical ring, which, when he turns it a particular way, makes him invisible, so that he can satisfy any desire he wishes without fear of punishment. When he discovers the power of the ring he kills the king, marries his wife and takes over the throne. And the moral of that story is?' Pythagoras asked Leonardo.

'Power corrupts,' Leonardo replied.

'Yes,' said Pythagoras.

Eventually the boat reached Crotone - a Greek colony in southern Italy.

Over the following months Pythagoras set up his religious community of men and women. The members of the Pythagorian sect showed a devoted attachment to each other, to the exclusion of those who did not belong to their ranks. There were even stories of secret symbols, by which members of the sect could recognise each other, even if they had never met before. The Pythagoreans became known for their theory of the transmigration of souls and also for their theory that numbers constitute the true nature of things. They performed purification rites and followed and developed various rules of living which they believed would enable their souls to achieve a higher rank among the gods.

Pythagoras was determined to implement the ideas of his teacher Pherecydes of Syros – the first Greek to teach a transmigration of souls. Pherecydes was Pythagoras's most "intimate" teacher. Pherecydes expounded his teaching on the soul in terms of a pentemychos ("five-nooks," or "five hidden cavities") — which the Pythagoreans symbolised as a five pointed star called a pentagram. They used this symbol to recognize other members and as a symbol of inner health and happiness, which they called Eudaimonia.

The Pythagoreans believed that a release from the "wheel of birth" was possible. They followed traditions and practices to purify the soul but at the same time they suggested a deeper idea of what such a purification might be. Music was used to purify the soul just like medicine was used to purge the body. The Pythagoreans believed that whole numbers and harmonic sounds are intimately connected in music and music and musical instruments can be mathematically quantified and described.

They followed Pythagoras's numerological belief that numbers were magical and ruled the universe. Everything had numerical relationships and it was up to the mind to seek and investigate the secrets of these relationships or have them revealed. They believed the number 3 was the noblest of all digits.

The Pythagoreans were well known for their vegetarianism, which they practised for religious, ethical and ascetic reasons, in particular the idea of the transmigration of souls into the bodies of other animals.

The Pythagorean code further restricted the diet of its followers, prohibiting the consumption or even touching of any sort of bean - due to their belief in the soul and the fact that beans obviously showed the potential for life. Some said that perhaps beans were banned because of the flatulence they caused.

After a few years enemies of the Pythagoreans set fire to Pythagoras' house, sending him running toward a bean field, where he halted, declaring that he would rather die than enter the field – whereupon his pursuers slit his throat.

Another story said that Pythagoras escaped to Metaponto in southern Italy, after he and his followers were persecuted and killed by authorities and the public, and there he starved himself to death.

At the first sign of trouble, we all escaped through Leonardo's time chest, although we didn't travel very far – in time or space. We ended up in Sicily in 200BC.

Leonardo took us to meet a great inventor called Archimedes, who looked very similar to Leonardo, with a long white beard. Archimedes recognised a kindred spirit in Leonardo and he showed him his notebooks, full of inventions such as a screw for lifting water, and a plan for reflecting the sun off mirrors in order to burn boats during warfare. Another was a giant claw which consisted of a crane-like arm from which a large metal grappling hook was suspended. When the claw was dropped onto an attacking ship the arm would swing upwards, lifting the ship out of the water and sinking it.

Leonardo was most excited by a machine Archimedes had designed which thousands of years later would be called the Antikythera mechanism (after the shipwreck in which it was found, near the Greek island of Antikythera.) It was one of the oldest computers ever made and consisted of a complex bronze gear mechanism which turned numerous dials. On one side, the dials form a calendar showing the positions of the sun, moon and the planets. On the other, the dials enable the prediction of solar and lunar eclipses. Greek astronomers had discovered by observation that the earth, moon and sun rotate in such a way that every 18 years 11 days they align to form an eclipse, with the moon directly between the earth and the sun blocking out its light. The mechanism was a model of the universe, and could be used to foresee the future positions of the planets.

After our visit with Archimedes, Leonardo made many notes, which he would use in his own inventions.

But we didn't stay long with Archimedes, as Leonardo said he wanted to meet a great ruler in India called Ashoka.

CHAPTER 9

India, 230BC

So we jumped in the time chest again and before you could shake a mouse's tail, we were in India, in 230BC.

We stood in the entrance to the emperor's palace, and the emperor was the man Leonardo wanted to meet – Ashoka. After waiting awhile, a servant beckoned us to follow him, and we were led to the throne room. As soon as Ashoka saw us, he walked straight up to Leonardo and said: 'I had a dream last night that you would come to me. Please, sit down.'

So we all sat down on large velvet cushions scattered on the floor. The throne room was full of intricately carved screens made of ivory and pink soapstone. Ashoka was wrapped in a deep purple silk robe, studded with rubies and emeralds.

Leonardo said: 'I have wanted to speak to you as I think we have something in common – a great burden of guilt. But you have managed to find redemption and atonement through Buddhism. I would like to find such peace of mind myself.'

Ashoka replied: 'It is possible to change. No-one is all bad or all good. The Chinese philosophy of Taoism uses a concept called "yin and yang", to describe how seemingly opposite or contrary forces are interconnected and interdependent in the natural world; and, how they give rise to each other as they interrelate to one another. Many natural dualities (such as female and male, dark and light, low and high, cold and hot, water and fire, life and death, and so on) are thought of as physical manifestations of the yin-yang concept. A symbol representing the principle of yin and yang is called the Taijitu (literally "diagram of the supreme ultimate")-

It is an S-shaped line that divides a circle into two equal parts - black and white with a black dot upon the white background, and a white dot upon the black background. This shows that inside the blackest, cruellest heart, there is a seed of goodness, and inside the purest, noblest heart, there is a seed of evil. I used to be evil, wicked, heartless, brutal, with a bad temper. I thought these were strengths that enabled me to become a great ruler and defeat my enemies. I managed to become king by getting rid of the legitimate heir to the throne, by tricking him into entering a pit filled with hot coals. I killed 99 of my brothers, sparing only one. I submitted my ministers to a test of loyalty and had 500 of them killed. I kept a harem of around 500 women. When a few of these women insulted me, I had the whole lot of them burnt to death. I built hell on earth - an elaborate and horrific torture chamber.

But my transformation came one day after the Kalinga War. The battle was a massive one and caused the deaths of more than 100,000 soldiers and many civilians who rose up in defence. When I was walking through the grounds of Kalinga after my conquest, rejoicing in my victory, I was moved by the number of bodies strewn there and the wails of the relatives of the dead. All I could see were burnt houses and scattered corpses. This sight made me sick and I cried:

"What have I done? If this is a victory, what's a defeat then? Is this a victory or a defeat? Is this justice or injustice? Is it gallantry or a rout? Is it valour to kill innocent children and women? Do I do it to widen the empire and for prosperity or to destroy the other's kingdom and splendour? One has lost her husband, someone else a father, someone a child, someone an unborn infant.... What's this debris of the corpses? Are these marks of victory or defeat? Are these vultures, crows, eagles the messengers of death or evil?"

After this I found Buddhism, and I tried to spread Buddhism as far as I could throughout the world – even to Rome, Greece, Egypt. I became a devotee of non violence, love, truth, tolerance and vegetarianism. I immediately abolished the unnecessary slaughter or mutilation of animals, branding and hunting animals for sport. I permitted limited hunting for consumption reasons but I also promoted vegetarianism. I constructed hospitals for animals too. I showed mercy to those imprisoned, allowing them to leave for the outside a day of the year. I attempted to raise the professional ambition of the common man and woman by building universities for study, and I allow women to be educated and enter religious institutions. I treat my subjects as equals regardless of their gender, religion, politics and caste.

The kingdoms surrounding mine, so easily overthrown, are instead well-respected allies. I follow the Buddhist principles of dharma - nonviolence, tolerance of all sects and opinions, obedience to parents, respect for the Brahmans and other religious teachers and priests, liberality towards friends, humane treatment of servants, and generosity towards all. All men and women are my children. I am like a father to them. As every father desires the good and the happiness of his children, I wish that all men and women should be happy always. I believe in herbal medicine for humans and animals, and wherever medical herbs and roots suitable for humans or animals are not available, I have had them imported and grown. Along roads I have had wells dug and trees planted for the benefit of humans and animals and I have had water transit and irrigation systems built for trade and agriculture.

Because I banned hunting, created veterinary clinics and eliminated meat eating on many holidays, my empire treats its animals as citizens who are as deserving of its protection as the human residents. I provide humanitarian help including doctors, hospitals, inns, wells, medical herbs and engineers to neighbouring countries. I have banned slavery, hunting, fishing, deforestation, the death sentence, and I have asked neighbouring countries to do the same. I recommend my people study and respect all religions. To harm another's religion is to harm one's own religion. I ask my people to live with harmony, peace, love, equality and tolerance. I do not aim to expand my territory and in my vast empire there is no evidence of mutiny or civil war.

I am against any discrimination among humans. I help students, the poor, orphans and the elderly with social, political and economic help. Hatred gives birth to hatred and a feeling of love gives birth to love and mercy. The happiness of people is the happiness of the ruler. The sword is not as powerful as love. Forgive me for speaking for so long. I do not mean to boast of my achievements. I am merely trying to show you how it is possible for someone to change. I look on my former self as a caterpillar in a chrysalis. I was blind. I could not truly see myself as others saw me. I had no empathy or compassion, so I did not care if people suffered because of my actions. Then suddenly I could see the reality, and feel others pain. Now I am a butterfly. It is never too late to change and seek redemption and atonement.'

Leonardo had tears falling down his cheeks. Ashoka put his hand on Leonardo's shoulder. He then held Leonardo's face in his hands and looked deeply into his eyes.

'I can see in your eyes you are a good man,' Ashoka said. 'Why do you feel so guilty?'

'A curse was put upon me. I was given a poison to drink – all the guilt of the world was in that bottle. Now there is a constant weight pressing down on my heart and soul. Sometimes it feels like a knife is being twisted in my stomach. I have been travelling through time in a quest to find the antidote,' Leonardo replied.

'I can help you,' Ashoka said. 'There is a tree near here called the Bodhi tree. This is where the Buddha achieved enlightenment. Do as he did. Sit under this tree and focus on your breathing. Eventually you will find complete insight into the cause of suffering, and the steps necessary to eliminate it. The Buddha called these the Four Noble Truths.

The First Noble Truth is understanding the nature of suffering – a lack of satisfaction pervading all forms of life, due to the fact that all forms of life are impermanent and constantly changing, and things never measure up to our expectations or standards. The Buddha acknowledged that there is both happiness and sorrow in the world, but he taught that even when we have some kind of happiness, it is not permanent; it is subject to change. And due to this unstable, impermanent nature of all things, everything we experience is said to have the quality of *dukkha* or unsatisfactoriness. Therefore unless we can gain insight into that truth, and understand what is really able to give us happiness, and what is unable to provide happiness, the experience of dissatisfaction will persist.

The Second Noble Truth is the origin of suffering – which is craving conditioned by ignorance. This craving is for pleasure, or to be something, or to be separated from painful feelings. Ignorance arises from a misunderstanding of the nature of the self and reality. Disturbing emotions are rooted in ignorance. They are like three poisons - misunderstanding of the nature of reality, attachment to pleasurable experiences, a fear of getting what we don't want, or not getting what we do want.

The Third Noble Truth is the ending of suffering and the causes of suffering – the ending of all the unsatisfactory experiences and their causes in such a way that they can no longer occur again. Once we have developed a genuine understanding of the causes of suffering, such as craving and ignorance, then we can completely eradicate these causes and thus be free from suffering. This leads to Nirvana – the ending of unhappiness. A temporary state of Nirvana can be said to occur whenever the causes of suffering (e.g. craving) have ceased in our mind.

The Fourth Noble Truth is the path to the ending of unhappiness. This path is called the Noble Eightfold Path and it is considered to be the essence of Buddhist practice. The eightfold path consists of: Right Understanding, Right Thought, Right Speech, Right Action, Right Livelihood, Right Effort, Right Mindfulness, and Right Concentration. While the first three truths are primarily concerned with understanding the nature of unhappiness (suffering, anxiety, stress) and its causes, the fourth truth presents a practical method for overcoming unhappiness. The path consists of a set of eight interconnected factors or conditions, that when developed together, lead to the ending of unhappiness. Thus, the eight items of the path are not to be understood as stages, in which each stage is completed before moving on to the next. Rather, they are to be understood as eight significant dimensions of one's behaviour—mental, spoken, and bodily—that operate in dependence on one another; taken together, they define a complete *path*, or way of living.

Through mastery of these truths, a state of supreme liberation, or Nirvana is believed to be possible for any being. The Buddha described Nirvāna as the perfect peace of a mind that's free from ignorance, greed, hatred and other afflictive states. Nirvana is also regarded as the "end of the world", in that no personal identity or boundaries of the mind remain. In such a state, a being is said to possess the Ten Characteristics belonging to every Buddha.'

We thanked Ashoka for what he had told us, and then walked a long way until we eventually reached the Bodhi tree. We all sat beneath it, focusing on our breathing. Cats are considered by Buddhists to be supreme masters of the art of Zen meditation. When Ashoka spoke I realised that I myself had already reached a state of Nirvana on many occasions whilst meditating. He did not have to teach me what to do, as meditation is part of a cat's natural behaviour. Cats look down in pity on humans, who are constantly rushing around, worrying, fretting. Cats know, as the Buddha did, that the best thing is to just be still and focus on your breathing.

After many hours had passed, I opened my eyes and although we were still sitting beneath a tree, it was a different tree, in a different time and place.

CHAPTER 10

Surrey, England, 1907

Now we were sitting underneath a beech tree and the temperature had dropped considerably. Instead of the bright blue sky and intense sun of India, there was a grey, cloudy, sky above. The cold air made me shiver.

'Where are we now?' I asked Leonardo.

'This is the Watts Chapel,' he replied and pointed to the building in front of us. Made of an orangey brick, it was circular, with terracotta Art Nouveau and Celtic designs around the top and door. These designs were of women, angels, animals, with sinuous lines and curves of plants and flowers woven between them. Leonardo stared hard at these designs.

'I think the medicine will be here', he said.

We went inside the chapel. It was very small, but filling all the walls, from top to bottom, were painted Art Nouveau figures of women and angels, brightly coloured in reds, blues, greens and gold. In front was a golden altar with intricately carved designs on it.

'What do all these symbols mean?' Louise asked.

'They represent quotations from the Bible,' Leonardo replied. 'From Isaiah 61 there is the quotation: "Good tidings unto the meek, bind up the broken hearted, proclaim liberty to the captives, comfort all that mourn", and from Apocrypha's Book of Wisdom there is: "The souls of the Righteous are in the hand of God – their hope is full of immortality". This Chapel was designed by a woman called Mary Fraser Tytler, who is now known under her married name of Mary Seton Watts. She married a famous artist called G.F.Watts. It is a shame she is not well known herself, but in England during this time it is not considered proper and feminine for a woman to be a professional artist – no matter how talented she is.'

Leonardo knelt down in front of the golden altar. One of the designs on it was a labyrinth. He traced the design with his finger. The sun started to peak through the clouds, and through the open door of the chapel a ray of sunshine streamed in, striking the altar and lighting it up. Gradually the ray of sunshine moved upwards, until it shone on a black picture above the altar. Now we could make out what the image was – a human figure in a hooded cloak, with a globe balancing on its lap. The globe started to rotate and the figure in the picture raised its hands above the globe. Still the face of the person was dark and hidden by the hood of the cloak, but suddenly we could see a pair of bright blue eyes staring out at us. The painted figures of women and angels on the walls started to move and dance. They stepped off the walls and flew out the door. We followed them, until we came to an Art Nouveau gravestone in the cemetery outside. On it was written the words: "No friendship dieth with death of any day, no true friendship lieth cold with lifeless clay. Though our boyhood's playtime be gone with summer's breath, no friendship fades with May-time, no friendship dies with death."

The angels beckoned us to follow them, and they pointed to a panel on the outside of the chapel. It contained raised terracotta heads of the woman who designed the chapel – Mary Watts. These heads had wings instead of arms, and held in each wing was a circle containing a symbol. One of the symbols was the scales of justice. Next to it was an owl, and above the owl was a key. The head next to the key had its eyes shut, but suddenly it opened its eyes, and with its wing, took the key and threw it down to Leonardo.

On the side of the key were written these words: "Throughout all eternity, I forgive you, you forgive me. – William Blake."

A red squirrel came up to us and said: 'Follow me.' So we all followed, across fields and paths, until we came to Leonardo's time travelling chest, which we climbed inside. We came out in the same place, but a different time – 2010. In front of us was a stately home – a huge Gothic castle built in brown stone, with turrets and gargoyles on the walls.

Leonardo knocked on the black front door, and it was opened by an old, crusty butler.

'I have come to see the owner of this house,' said Leonardo.

'Do you have an appointment?' the butler asked.

'No,' Leonardo replied.

'Wait here', the butler said, and he closed the door. We waited for about 10 minutes until the butler came back.

'Lord Fart of Fartington has agreed to see you. Please enter.' And with a withered, bony hand the butler beckoned us in. He looked at us like we were something that had just been dragged out of a cesspit. Wrinkling up his nose as if we smelt very bad, he told us to follow him.

After walking through many dark, narrow corridors, we were eventually led into a room in which a small man sat in a large chair. He looked like a stuffed pigeon, with a small moustache and grey hair. He was 90 years old and married to an 18 year old lap dancer from Texas.

'What can I do for you?' Lord Fart said.

'I have been given a key and I have been led to believe it may fit something inside this house,' Leonardo replied.

'Who led you to believe that?' Lord Fart asked.

'A red squirrel,' Leonardo replied.

'Are you mad? You look mad.' Lord Fart said.

Leonardo showed the key to Lord Fart, who squinted at it.

'Doesn't ring any bells with me I'm afraid. I think you are barking up the wrong tree on this one,' he said.

Lord Fart gazed at the glass of whisky he was holding in his hand, and then started to proceed to tell us a very long, boring story about a key he lost once, many years ago in his youth. Just as I was about to nod off, he dropped his glass on the floor.

Annoyed by this mishap, Lord Fart suddenly barked at us: 'If you will excuse me, I am very busy, and I do not have time to waste conversing with lunatics.' Lord Fart waved his hand dismissively at us, so we left.

As we reached the hall, Lord Fart's wife flounced downstairs in a skimpy dress.

'Hi. You look like a fun bunch of guys.' She said in a Texan drawl, and flashed a dazzling white smile at us.

'We have just been told to leave by Lord Fart,' Leonardo said.

'Oh, really, that's a shame. Why don't you come upstairs to my room. I'm bored out of my brain in this mausoleum,' she said.

So we followed her up the stairs, where she led us into a large, palatial room, full of thick, plush white carpets and gold trimmed furniture. In one corner of the room was a grand piano. I sat down on the piano stool, put my paws on the keys and started to play one of my own compositions – something with a hint of Gershwin and Liszt. Everyone applauded when I'd finished. I then started to play some jazz and boogie-woogie and everyone started to dance. Jerry the Meerkat popped up from nowhere and joined in the dancing, as did the Trade Union Leader Mouse. It's so hard to keep the riff raff out these days.

Exhausted after our dancing we decided to relax by playing Monopoly. Lady Fart did not consider it strange that a cat could play Monopoly (and win) – a feature of her which I liked very much.

After my victory Leonardo explained to her about the key and she rummaged around in the back of her wardrobe until she pulled out a small wooden box. She gave it to Leonardo, he put the key in the lock, and amazingly enough, it opened. Inside the box was a small bottle, with a liquid inside. Leonardo took the cork out of the top, and drank the liquid. He then fainted, but came round again a few minutes later.

'I think I have drunk the antidote. I feel a great weight has lifted from my heart,' Leonardo said.

'Why don't you stay the night?' Lady Fart asked. She summoned the butler and instructed him to make arrangements for us to sleep over.

'Can I ask you a personal question?' Louise asked Lady Fart.

'Sure,' said Lady Fart.

'Why did you marry Lord Fart?' Louise asked.

'Oh, because he's rich of course. It wasn't because of his sparkling personality or good looks, that's for sure! He's 90, so I figured I'd only have to put up with him for a few years at the most, and then once he kicks the bucket, I'll inherit all this. But unfortunately he seems to be fitter than I thought, and

I don't know how much longer I can stand it in this freezing cold, draughty house. In fact I don't know how anyone lives in Britain at all. No sunshine and constant rain, cold, wind, all year round. I suppose that's why everyone is so miserable in this country,' said Lady Fart.

'Life is a never-ending series of disappointments', Leonardo said. We all nodded in agreement and eventually went into our separate bedrooms. I slept at the foot of Leonardo's bed, and Crystal slept at the foot of Louise's bed next door.

After listening to Leonardo snore for a considerable length of time, he suddenly sat bolt upright in bed, staring wildly in front of him. I turned to where he was looking, and my fur stood up on end like I'd been plugged into an electric light socket.

Charles Dickens was standing in front of us. He was dressed in a dark brown jacket with a red geranium in his button hole paired with cream coloured trousers. His face was thin and lined. Under his bright blue eyes were dark circles, bags and wrinkles. A straggling, grizzled beard pointed down from his chin. Although his beard was mostly grey, the hair on his head was dark brown, in soft waves.

He walked over to Leonardo and said: 'All my life there has been a great big hole in my heart. I never felt like my parents loved me or wanted me. They sent me to work in a blacking factory when I was a child. I felt like an orphan, thrown into hell. When I became an adult I wanted to be an actor instead of a writer, but a cold prevented me from auditioning.'

Leonardo said: 'If you'd been an actor, you would be forgotten by now, but as a writer you are immortal and will live forever. Fate steers us in the right direction, without us even being aware of it. The things we think of as failures, dead ends, missed opportunities, is really just Fate steering us away from the wrong direction and into the right direction.'

Dickens said: 'Yes, you are right. I became a writer to exorcise my demons and let them escape in disguise. I was never at rest when I was alive. I couldn't sleep, so I would walk the streets of London all night. I was like a toy that had been wound up and couldn't stop. Now I'm dead I still can't rest, as I feel guilty for having an affair. I separated from my wife, but I was too afraid of harming my reputation to divorce her. So I couldn't marry my young mistress, even though she gave birth to my child, who died aged two years old.

When I was travelling on a train with my mistress, the train crashed and 10 people died. I didn't want to attend the inquest as I didn't want it to be known I was travelling with my mistress. Some poor railwayman called Benge took the blame for the crash, as he read the timetable wrong and thought he had longer to mend the railway tracks before the train came. He was sentenced to 9 months hard labour in prison and later the guilt made him go mad and he died in a lunatic asylum. His boss was also found guilty, but because he had money and contacts, he wasn't sent to prison. The real guilty party was the railway company for not maintaining the tracks properly. I hate injustice and have fought it all my life. If I had gone to the inquest I could have saved Benge from prison, but I stayed away in order to protect my reputation.

I realise now what a hypocrite I was. I put my reputation and career above everything else – including the happiness of my wife and mistress and of some poor railwayman. Benge made one small mistake – reading a timetable wrong, and that led to a train crash in which ten people died. And for that one small mistake he was sent to prison and went mad, dying in a lunatic asylum. The guilt killed him, but he had no reason to feel guilty. I felt no guilt for my mistakes when I was alive, but now I do. Of course we all make mistakes. I should never have married my wife, but once I realised she was not the right person for me, I should have divorced her and married my mistress, but if I had done that it would have ruined my career and reputation. When I died I felt the pain I had caused my wife and mistress, and the railwayman, and now I regret it so much. I know you have felt guilt and you have found the antidote. Can you give it to me?'

Leonardo said: 'A mistake is something you didn't intend to do – where you couldn't foresee the consequences of your actions. A mistake can lead to terrible consequences and even death, but if you did not intend to harm or kill, you cannot blame yourself.'

Leonardo held Dickens hand. A tear fell from Dickens eye. Leonardo caught the tear on his finger and put it in the bottle he had drunk from earlier. There was still a tiny bit of liquid left in it. Leonardo shook the bottle and told Dickens to drink it, which he did. Dickens breathed a sigh of relief, said 'thank you', and disappeared.

The next morning Lady Fart came into our room, carrying a suitcase. She said: 'I've decided to leave this dump and go back to America. Lord Fart went crazy last night when he found out I'd let you all stay over. I can't stand that guy any longer. Do you want to come with me? I've decided to go to California.'

'Well, yes, I've never been to America.' Leonardo said.

CHAPTER 11

Monterey, California, USA, 2010

We were tired after our very long flight so we decided to get a breath of fresh air by walking along the sea front at Monterey Bay. Beneath the bright blue sky was a wide azure sea. The heat of the sun wrapped itself around me like a blanket. The brightness of the sun dazzled and almost blinded me. I breathed in the salty air. Sunlight sparkled on the sea like diamonds. Floating in the water were cat-like creatures, lying on their back, grooming themselves, rubbing their eyes with their paws, washing behind their ears, yawning, eating. They were sea otters, but were doing a good impression of cats that could swim. One of the sea otters waved to me and I waved back. It swam over to me, yawned and said: 'Why don't you join us?'

'I can't swim,' I replied.

'Really, you must be a different species. Tourists!.' He swam off and grabbed the paw of another sea otter. Holding hands, they floated away.

Leonardo stood in front of us all – me, Lady Fart, Crystal, Louise, and said:

'Now I have found the antidote to my guilt, I feel like my journey has come to an end. I am free from the great weight that was pressing down on my heart and soul. Now I can return back to my own time and place – Italy in the 1500s. Tom, will you come with me?'

'Of course,' I said, and jumped up into Leonardo's arms. He held me tight and I licked his face and purred as he stroked me.

Louise said: 'Me and Lady Fart had a long talk on the plane over here, and we've decided to stay in California and write a self-help book about men and how to survive them.'

'I am sure it will be a bestseller,' Leonardo said. 'And what about you Crystal? What do you want to do?'

Crystal looked deeply into my eyes and said: 'I think I have fallen in love with Tom. I would like to join him, if it's possible.'

'Of course,' Leonardo said.

I leapt down from Leonardo's arms. Crystal came up to me and rubbed the side of her face against mine. We both purred and licked each other's faces. Amorous times ahead – at last!

THE END

Printed in Poland
by Amazon Fulfillment
Poland Sp. z o.o., Wrocław